Fart Squad #3: Unidentified Farting Objects

For information address HarperCollins Children's Books, a division of HarperCollins Publishers, 195 Broadway, New York, NY 10007.
www.harpercollinschildrens.com

Library of Congress Control Number: 2015943571
ISBN 978-0-06-236633-7 (trade bdg.)—ISBN 978-0-06-229049-6 (pbk.)

Design by Victor Joseph Ochoa
15 16 17 18 19 CG/RRDH 10 9 8 7 6 5 4 3 2 1
❖
First Edition

UNIDENTIFIED FARTING OBJECTS

by SEAMUS PILGER
illustrated by STEPHEN GILPIN

HARPER
An Imprint of HarperCollins*Publishers*
full fathom five

CHAPTER ONE

"I'm not kidding—it was a UFO, I promise!"

Darren Stonkadopolis had called an emergency meeting of the Fart Squad and now he was standing in front of its three other members at the empty drive-in. The drive-in was closed for the season so it was the perfect spot for their practice sessions. He was trying to tell them about the close encounter of the stinky kind he'd had the night before.

"Don't be ridiculous!" said Tina Heiney, decked out in a spotless secret Fart Squad outfit. "What did it look like, a *flying saucer*?" She could barely get through that sentence without laughing, then snorting with pure glee. Tina might have looked like a little princess, but a lot of what came out of her was royally inappropriate.

"I'm not sure exactly," Darren admitted. "I didn't really stop to look at it. But it was definitely coming after me. Another few minutes and I would have been abducted for sure!"

"You positive about that?" Juan-Carlos Finkelstein asked, grinning. Darren could tell by his tone that the lanky class clown was winding up to tell another one of his jokes. "Maybe they just wanted directions," he started, then paused for comedic effect. "You know, to the Big Dipper!"

"Yes—I'm positive about it!" Darren said. He was used to Juan-Carlos trying to be funny any chance he got, but this was no laughing matter. "I'd heard all the recent reports and sightings, and I didn't take them very seriously either. But I barely got away last night. What if that UFO comes back for me? And what if you guys are with me?"

Finally Darren said something that got the group's attention.

"At first all I noticed was a bright white glare looming over me," he continued. "A storm was brewing and so I figured it was just a flash of lightning. But the light, along with an overpowering, stomach-turning odor, followed me for several minutes. I was a little scared to look up at the sky, but when I did, I spotted a large glowing object descending through the clouds, which proceeded to follow me until I found cover in a porta-potty." At this, his friends broke out into gales of laughter, which he ignored. He would probably laugh too if he imagined what Walter or Tina would look like crouched inside a stall, hiding from nothing more than a pool of light.

"Luckily, it started to rain," he continued, "and the spacecraft retreated, but who knows where to and for how long?"

"Please!" Tina said, unconvinced. "It was probably just a helicopter or something. *Everybody* knows there's no such thing as UFOs."

"I beg to differ," Walter Turnip said. Round and plump, he seldom used a simple word when there was a bigger one available (or ate a small portion when a bigger one was at hand), but Darren appreciated Walter coming to his defense. "Given the sheer, incalculable immensity of the cosmos, it is statistically unlikely that only our own native Earth would give birth to sentient life-forms," he said as he devoured a plate of hot dogs. "Mere probability dictates that we are not alone in the universe."

"I suppose," Tina admitted. "But that doesn't mean that honest-to-goodness space aliens are taking joyrides over Buttzville." She rolled her eyes at the very notion. "You were probably just seeing things."

"No way," Darren said. "I know what I saw. And I'm not the only one. There's been a bunch of UFO sightings around here lately. And guess what? Some of the eyewitnesses were *nose* witnesses, too. They reported

smelling the same peculiar odor when the UFO appeared."

"What kind of odor, exactly?" Tina asked.

Darren tried to describe it. "A gross, poopy smell . . . like a titanic toot."

"In other words," Juan-Carlos said with a smirk, "an Unidentified Farting Object?"

Tina peered suspiciously at Walter.

"You can refrain from looking at me," he protested, even though his farts were big and powerful enough to propel him through the air like a human-sized blimp. "It was not yours truly, I assure you!"

"I never thought it was," Darren said. "But what are we going to do about the *real* aliens?" He was frustrated by his friends' failure to take this seriously. "We could be facing an invasion from outer space!"

Tina shrugged. "I still think you've seen too many silly sci-fi movies," she told Darren.

"I can't believe I'm wasting a perfectly good Saturday on this."

"Laugh all you like," Darren said, "but as team leader I say we need to practice our powers some more in case that UFO comes back."

"I guess some extra practice couldn't hurt," Juan-Carlos said. "Since we're here anyway."

Walter finished the last of his hot dogs. "I'm certainly amenable to any impromptu exercises . . . if there are burritos involved."

"Why not?" Tina sighed. "This afternoon is already shot."

"That's the spirit!" Darren said, relieved that the Squad was finally listening to him. He dashed into the abandoned snack bar and returned moments later with a tray of reheated burritos. "Time to fuel up. Dig in!"

"With the utmost pleasure!" Walter licked his lips in anticipation. As far as

Darren knew, Walter was the only member of the Fart Squad, and probably the human race, who actually enjoyed eating the soggy, greasy burritos. Anyone else might have been grossed out by their power alone, because they sure didn't get so potent from tasting good. If they tasted good, they'd have been gobbled up, not left over for the lunch ladies to keep reheating in the microwave day in, day out, to the point of radioactivity. But Walter Turnip didn't care.

Walter eagerly wolfed down one burrito after another until his belly filled with gas and he became so rotund that he lifted off the ground like a hot-air balloon. "Be careful to keep out of sight," Darren coached him. "Don't fly higher than the trees or movie screen."

The Science Behind Walter's Behind

Walter circled above the drive-in, propelled by jets of gas from his rear end, while Darren and the others each helped themselves to a burrito—with a lot less enthusiasm. Tina nibbled at hers delicately, using a bib and napkin to keep from making a mess. Juan-Carlos washed his down with a bottle of chocolate milk to kill the taste.

"Ugh." Darren forced down another bite. "Why couldn't we get our powers from something yummier? Like doughnuts or jelly beans or something?"

"Then we'd be the Cavity Squad," Juan-Carlos joked. "But wait until I show you how long I can delay my stink bombs these days. Watch this!"

He dashed across the gravel lot until he was more than a hundred yards away from the others, halfway between the snack bar and the thirty-foot-tall movie screen at the far end of the drive-in. At his signal, Darren called up the stopwatch app on his phone. Then Juan-Carlos squatted and grimaced in concentration, like he was ripping a big one.

Darren didn't hear or smell anything, but he hadn't expected to. Juan-Carlos's farts were like time bombs, going off after he dealt them. He'd been working on delaying the explosions for as long as he could manage. Darren started the timer on his phone.

"Don't hold your breath waiting for this one!" Juan-Carlos hollered back at them.

"I'm going for a personal best!"

He sure wasn't kidding. By the time he'd run all the way back across the lot to rejoin the rest of the Squad, the stink bomb *still* hadn't gone off.

Darren was impressed. Tina not so much.

"How do we know this wasn't just a dud?" she asked. "You sure you actually did anything?"

"Look who's talking," Juan-Carlos replied. "Little Miss Silent-But-Deadly."

Her eyes narrowed. "You know," she said sweetly, "I need to practice, too."

Juan-Carlos gulped and backed away from the tiny little girl, whose sneaky stealth farts were potent enough to knock out a fellow Fart Squad member.

"Whoa," Darren said. "Let's play nice here. Remember, there is no *I* in Fart Squad—"

A foul odor washing over the drive-in interrupted his pep talk. The sour smell seemed to come out of nowhere.

"Not bad," Tina congratulated Juan-Carlos. "If you're impressed by that kind of thing."

"Um, I wish I could take credit." Juan-Carlos looked puzzled. "But mine are usually much louder, you know?"

"It wasn't you!" Darren blurted. He recognized the ominous smell instantly. "The UFO! It's back!"

Darren peered anxiously at the sky, just in time to be blinded by a sudden, all-too-familiar glare. The brightness cut through the cloudy, overcast sky, lighting up the drive-in as though it were the middle of summer. Walter swooped down from above, shouting and waving his arms.

"We are not alone!"

A glowing object descended from the clouds, accompanied by gusts of pungent exhaust that stank to high heaven. The smell was vaguely fartlike, but Darren still couldn't quite place it.

"See!" he said. "I told you I wasn't joking!"

CHAPTER TWO

"Okay," Tina admitted, "maybe you weren't imagining things."

As the UFO came in for a landing, Darren shielded his eyes with his hand to get a better look at the large glowing object. About the size of a mobile home, it was made entirely of tinted glass panes lit up from inside.

Kind of like a greenhouse, Darren thought.

Walter touched down on the gravel beside Darren and the others. He looked relieved to be back on solid ground.

"As you can see," he pointed out, "I am most definitely *not* the UFO in question!"

Spewing clouds of noxious exhaust, the glowing glass ship landed inside the

drive-in, several yards away from Darren and his friends. A door slid open and a landing ramp descended to the ground. Just like the night before, visions of slimy tentacles, drooling jaws, and death rays invaded Darren's mind. He finished off his burrito in a hurry and clenched his butt to hold on to his farts, just in case he needed them to defend Earth. "Bring it on," he muttered.

But, to his surprise, the aliens exiting the UFO looked like . . .

Flowers?

Bright-yellow sunflowers to be exact. They glided toward the Squad on graceful green stems. Rings of sunny petals surrounded their disklike faces. Leafy branches served as their limbs. They were each about as tall as a child and gave off a delicate scent that reminded Darren of his mother's perfume.

"Why, they're almost as pretty as I am!" Tina beamed happily. "I approve!"

Juan-Carlos, on the other hand, sounded almost disappointed. "What kind of aliens are these? I was expecting something gross and creepy . . . not a walking bouquet!"

"More like extraflorestrials," Walter said. "Possibly an alien variety of *Helianthus annuus.*"

Everyone gave him blank looks.

"Sunflowers," he explained. "Or maybe Star Flowers, in this case."

"Star Flowers," Tina repeated, all dreamy-eyed and enchanted.

Darren had to admit that the alien flowers did not look particularly scary. He'd heard of nasty, man-eating plants before, but the Star Flowers appeared more decorative than dangerous. He sniffed the air where traces of the UFO's exhaust scent still lingered.

"Why does their ship smell like farts?" he wondered.

"Fertilizer," Walter corrected him, "not flatulence. Although you can be forgiven for confusing the odors. Many varieties of fertilizer manifest a distinctly fecal aroma. Anyone who has ever lived near a large agricultural complex can testify to that."

"You mean it smells like poo," Darren translated. "Makes sense, I guess. They are plants, after all."

The Star Flowers approached the kids

warily. Shiny black eyes the size of sunflower seeds looked over Darren and his friends. Their mouths were just tiny slits. They seemed perfectly harmless.

"I don't see any weapons," he observed.

"Nope," Juan-Carlos admitted. "We're talking pistils, not pistols."

Tina groaned again.

Darren stepped forward to meet the aliens. He swallowed hard.

"Hello?"

"Don't get too close, Darren." Juan-Carlos hung back with the others. "They're just flowers, I know, but . . . be careful."

But *careful* was not a word that had ever been used to describe Darren, who had a bad habit of rushing into situations without thinking. As leader of the Fart Squad, he felt it was his duty to check out the aliens and represent for his crew.

"Um, welcome to Earth?" He wasn't quite sure what to say, or even if the aliens could understand him. "Live long and prosper? May the Force be with you? *¿Habla inglés?*"

One of the Star Flowers was a few inches taller than the other aliens and stood out in front of the rest of them. The bizarre being paused in front of Darren and tilted its head curiously. A fresh whiff of perfume tickled Darren's nose, but the Star Flower didn't reply to the human greeting.

"Can you understand me?" Darren asked. Resorting to sign language, he pointed first at himself, then up at the sky. "Me . . . Darren. You . . . from out there?"

The aroma from the Star Flower grew stronger.

"Ah, you perceive that mellifluous bouquet?" Walter said, sniffing deeply. "Note the subtle shifts in its fragrance."

"So what?" Juan-Carlos asked impatiently. "I mean, they smell nice and all, and I'm glad they're not eating us, but are they shy or something? Why aren't they saying anything?"

A crazy idea hit Darren.

"Maybe they are," he said. "They're flowers, right? Maybe they communicate through smells instead of words."

"You mean they have extra*scent*sory perception?" Juan-Carlos joked.

Tina groaned again. "Probably just as well they can't understand you."

"I'm serious," Darren said. "When have you ever heard of a talking flower? Maybe they 'talk' to each other in fragrances instead of words."

"Then perhaps we can reply via some olfactory emissions of our own," Walter suggested. "More than most people, we are certainly capable of generating very perceptible aromas."

"And then some," Juan-Carlos said.

"I'm not sure that's a good idea," Darren cautioned. His own stomach was rumbling impatiently, thanks to the burritos, but he kept the gas locked up tight. "Pleasant smells are one thing, but who knows what a fart means to them. They might take any rude smells as insults . . . or a declaration of war!"

"Good point," Juan-Carlos agreed.

Darren decided to stick to the basics. He took another step forward and held out his hand.

"Peace?"

The Star Flower appeared to be considering Darren's outstretched hand. After a moment's pause, it extended a leafy green tendril toward him.

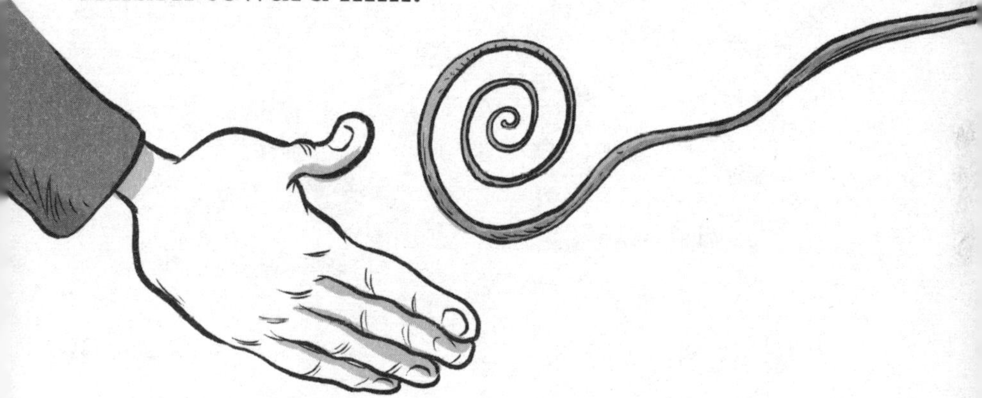

"Yes!" Darren said hopefully. "That's right. We just want to make friends with you!"

And then, just as Darren thought he was about to be the first kid on Earth to establish contact with actual beings from outer space, a loud, putrid fart, strong enough to make grown men weep, exploded right in the middle of the Star Flowers. . . .

Oh no! Darren thought.

In all the excitement, they had completely forgotten about Juan-Carlos's stink bomb!

CHAPTER THREE

The explosive fart went off right where Juan-Carlos had planted it before. The Star Flowers were knocked to the ground, overwhelmed by the sneak attack. Their faces twisted in shock. Their branches flailed wildly.

"Oops!" Juan-Carlos said. "Talk about bad timing!"

Ten minutes, forty-two seconds, Darren noted after checking his stopwatch. *A new record all right. Just our luck!*

Swaying atop their stems, the Star Flowers managed to get upright again, glaring at the kids with their glossy black eyes. A new smell wafted over the Squad members. It was harsh—neither fartlike nor floral. It smelled . . . angry.

Darren gulped. Could he make them understand that this was just an accident, or did they think they had been ambushed on purpose?

"Sorry about that!" he called out urgently. He raised his hands and tried to look contrite. It was an expression that worked on his teachers and parents sometimes. He hoped the Star Flowers would be just as forgiving. "Our bad!"

He half-expected the startled aliens to leave and never come back. Or, worse yet, zap them all with death rays in retaliation. But instead the Star Flowers began to . . . *change.*

Cheery yellow petals turned gray and jagged. Graceful green stems transformed into an ugly shade of purple as they turned twisted and gnarly before his eyes. Thorny vines sprouted like tentacles. Bulging eyes turned bloodred. Their mouths turned into snapping jaws, like Venus flytraps'. And instead of smelling fragrant and flowery, the aliens now gave off a stomach-turning stench that rivaled anything the Fart Squad had ever dealt

out. The smell was so bad that Darren had to put his hand over his mouth and nose.

"Ugh!" Tina wrinkled her nose in disgust. "They smell like . . . well, you guys. No offense."

"I don't understand," Juan-Carlos said. "What's happening?"

Darren had seen enough monster movies to figure it out.

"The radioactive fart!" he realized. "It's *mutating* them! Turning them into monstrous . . . Stink Weeds!"

"An extremely troubling metamorphosis," Walter agreed, floating a few inches above the gravel. "Perhaps best contemplated from a greater distance?"

Probably not a bad idea, Darren thought, but before he could move, a spiky vine whipped out and snagged him by his wrist.

"Ouch!" he yelped as sharp thorns dug through his sleeve into his skin. "Let go!"

But the vine tightened around his wrist so that he couldn't pry it loose and yanked his arm, dragging him even closer to the Stink Weeds. Sticky green sap dripped from their jaws. "Let me go!" he hollered again. "We didn't mean to weed-ify you! It was an accident!"

More vines entangled him, rooting him to the ground, even as the rest of the Fart Squad rushed to his rescue. Twisting around, Darren aimed his butt at the vines to try to defend

himself. His stomach rumbled in anticipation. A blazing-hot fart was ready to go.

Careful, he thought, not wanting to burn the aliens to a crisp. *Just a warning shot for now.*

Darren's farts burned superhot. A scorching *blaat* singed the seat of his pants—but seemed to have no effect on the clinging vines. Struggling against them, he heard Tina charging fearlessly into battle.

"Leave him alone, you revolting weeds!"

Darren didn't hear her fart, but he never does. Tina's silent gas attacks snuck up on people. Darren hoped they worked on angry aliens, too. But the stealth fart just seemed to mutate the Stink Weeds even more, making them grow bigger and spikier. Vines snared Tina now. She squirmed, unable to break free as fresh sap oozed down their stems and onto the trapped kids.

"Yuck!!" she shouted in disgust. "Let us go!"

Darren spotted Walter and Juan-Carlos right behind her.

"Watch out!" he called in warning. "Our farts just seem to make them stronger!"

"Seriously?" Juan-Carlos skidded to a halt, just out of reach of the furious Weeds. "So what are we supposed to do? Call Lawn Doctor?"

Walter hovered a few feet above Juan-Carlos. "I confess my horticultural skills leave something to be desired!"

The Stink Weeds turned their faces toward the other boys. Dark-purple pollen sprayed like powder from the Weeds' open jaws. The pollen blew over the kids, who began coughing and sneezing uncontrollably. Their eyes watered. Their noses ran. Snot streamed down their faces. . . .

The sticky pollen clung to their clothes. Darren watched in alarm as the Stink Weeds slithered toward his friends. Greedy vines reached out for them.

"Run for it!" Darren ordered the others. "Save yourselves!"

"Forget it—*achoo!*" Juan-Carlos could barely speak, he was sneezing so hard. He tried to wipe the pollen off himself but just ended up smearing it all over. "We're a team—*cough, cough!* We're not going to leave—*achoo!*"

"My sentiments precisely," Walter said. "One for all and all for . . . *achoo!*"

A violent sneeze sent him shooting backward like a leaky balloon. He collided with Juan-Carlos, knocking them both out of harm's way.

“Don’t be stupid!” Darren shouted over the sneezing. “You need to get out of here before these nasty weeds get you, too! Remember: he who farts and runs lives to fart another day!” Jagged vines squeezed his ribs and ankles.

Juan-Carlos grabbed on to Walter’s leg as Walter’s farts blasted them up into the sky. Juan-Carlos got a faceful of gas, but Darren figured it beat being captured by mutant plants from outer space . . . sort of.

The vines grew at a frightening rate, climbing upward, straining to capture the fleeing humans. A stink bomb exploded in the air behind Juan-Carlos.

"Sorry," he apologized. "That one just slipped out."

The radioactive gas sparked another weedy growth spurt. The vines snagged Juan-Carlos's foot. "Let go, you grabby greenery!" He kicked off his sneaker before the vine could climb any higher up his leg.

The shoe fell to the ground not far from where Darren and Tina were snared.

"Keep flying!" Darren yelled. "Don't worry about us!"

"Speak for yourself," Tina muttered.

The vines yanked Darren and Tina off

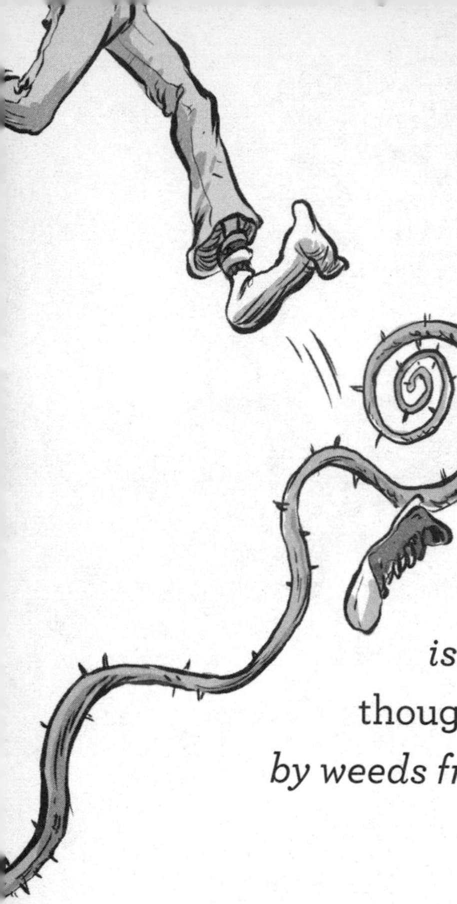

their feet and toward the waiting spaceship. Darren grunted as he bounced over the rough gravel surface.

I can't believe this is really happening, he thought. *We're being abducted by weeds from outer space!*

CHAPTER FOUR

"Juan-Carlos is never going to let me hear the end of this," Tina said as she and Darren were dragged through the open doorway into the spaceship.

"*If* we ever see him again," Darren said. "Or anybody else we know!"

At first, the inside of the UFO smelled like a garden, full of pretty aromas, but the Stink Weeds' foul odor quickly polluted the air. Darren tried to breathe through his mouth instead of his nose, but that just seemed to make it worse.

"These aliens are so rude," Tina said. "Can't they even bother to keep the air fresh for company?"

"Maybe they like it this way?" Darren said.

The UFO's interior, like its exterior, resembled a greenhouse. In front of the control panel, there were flower pots where there should have been seats. Dirt covered the decks. Glass walls let in sunlight—and Darren could only watch as the ship took off into the sky. Within minutes, they were thousands of feet above Buttzville.

He was starting to think that he was definitely going to be late for dinner.

The Stink Weeds led them into a laboratory deep inside the ship. Sunlamps were built into the ceiling, while pruning shears, clippers, hoses, and other gardening tools hung on the walls, along with other, more alien equipment that Darren couldn't identify. He wasn't sure he wanted to know what they were for.

"What do you think they're going to do to us?" he asked Tina anxiously. "What if they want revenge on us for turning them into weeds?"

"Let's not assume the worst," Tina said.

"I can't help it." Anxiety caused his stomach to churn unhappily, the pressure growing more and more uncomfortable. "What if they want to use us as lab rats? Or fertilizer?"

"They wouldn't dare," Tina said. "I'm much too refined for that!"

The vines released the two of them, finally, but they were outnumbered and thousands of feet in the air. And unlike Walter, neither Darren nor Tina could fly.

They were trapped. They were doomed.

The tallest Stink Weed leaned toward the two prisoners, giving off a revolting stench that made Darren's stomach turn. Its vines twitched.

"I'm sorry," Darren said. "I still can't understand you. I don't speak stink."

The Weed scratched its head as though it was mulling over the situation. Moments later, a blinking device that looked like the 3D printer that Darren had seen on a field trip to the Buttzville Science Center turned on. The machine hummed briefly and spit out two pairs of shiny, silver . . . underpants?

The Big Weed hooked the shorts with a vine and tossed them at the kids, who peered at the unusual underpants in confusion. Darren had no idea what was going on. Of all the bizarre possibilities he'd been dreading, this had not been one of them. Brain eating, sure, but alien underwear?

The Weeds rustled impatiently.

"I think they want us to put them on," Darren guessed.

Tina picked up the smaller shorts by one corner, holding them out and away from her with her fingertips. "You first," she said.

"Okay."

Darren pulled the crinkly metallic shorts over his pants. He figured he looked like a doofus, wearing the underpants on the outside, but right now that was the least of his worries. The Stink Weeds were calling the shots, so he and Tina had to play along.

"Your turn," he said.

Tina groaned. "This is not a good look for me."

She reluctantly pulled on the shorts as well. "Don't say a word," she warned Darren before addressing the Stink Weeds. "Now what?"

The printer hummed again and produced two pairs of matching silver nose plugs. As before, the Big Weed passed the plugs to the puzzled kids, who put them in without knowing why. The plugs were a perfect fit. Darren hoped they weren't designed to suck his brains out.

"Can you understand us now?" the Big Weed said. "Pass gas if you understand."

Static tingled Darren's nostrils, but he could "hear" the Stink Weed talking now. Darren and Tina exchanged startled looks. He could tell by her expression that she could understand the alien, too.

"The nose plugs!" Darren exclaimed. "They must be translating their smell into words."

"They tickle," she said. "I hope they're properly sanitized."

"Do not reply with your tongues," the Big Weed instructed. "Transmit your thoughts by scent alone."

"Um, okay." Darren was not entirely sure how to do that. He unclenched his butt just a little, for fear of strengthening the Weeds with another high-powered fart, and let out the smallest puff of gas he could manage.

HELLO? TESTING? TESTING. . . .

"No need to shout," the Big Weed said. "Please adjust the volume on your translator shorts."

Darren found a dial on the waistband and turned it to a lower setting. He hoped it would help control the intensity of his toots . . . as long as he didn't let loose all the way.

LiKe tHiS? he farted.

"Much better," the big Weed confirmed. "The translator shorts will convert your gaseous emissions into proper speech, while the nasal receivers will allow you to make sense of our scents. No pun intended." He pointed a thorny vine at them. "Greetings, human specimens."

Specimens?

Darren didn't like the sound of that.

PLEASED TO MEET YOU, Tina tooted politely. WHO ARE YOU AND WHERE DO YOU COME FROM?

"Call me . . . Doctor Thorn," the Weed replied. "I am the commander and chief scientist of this vessel, the Flying Astral Research/Telecommunication Ship (F.A.R.T.S.). My crew and I are an advance scouting party from the planet Botanica, many light-years from here. We were exploring this solar system, searching for signs of intelligent life, when our sensors detected unusually powerful smells coming from your planet. We mistook the odors for a distress signal from an advanced civilization similar to our own, so we traced them to the locality you call 'Buttzville.' But we were unable to pinpoint the source of the unique smells until today."

ER, THAT WOULD BE US, I GUESS, Darren squeezed out. It was kind of embarrassing to realize that their farts could be smelled all the way from space, but it sounded like this was all just a big misunderstanding. SORRY, FALSE ALARM. WE'RE NOT IN DISTRESS, I PROMISE!

YES, WE'RE JUST FINE, Tina added. THANKS FOR YOUR PROMPT RESPONSE, BUT WE DON'T NEED YOUR HELP. REALLY.

"You think that matters now?" Doctor Thorn gave off a disturbing new odor, which

smelled like wicked laughter. He waved his gnarled vines around. "Look how your strange human vapor has transformed us. We're not weak, caring Flowers anymore. We're Weeds now . . . and you're going to help us spread across the galaxy!"

Darren realized that the aliens had turned ugly on the inside as well. I don't understand. What do you need us for?

"To transform the rest of our people into Weeds, of course," Doctor Thorn gloated. "Our mother ship is waiting for us just outside your solar system. Once your alien gases turn our entire expedition into Weeds, we will do the same to Botanica, and then infest the entire universe!"

But I don't want to get dragged to another planet, Tina protested. I like Earth just fine, thank you very much!

Darren knew how she felt. This was

getting worse and worse. He knew he had to think fast if they ever wanted to see their friends and families again.

WAIT! he stalled. WE CAN'T FART ENOUGH TO TRANSFORM YOUR ENTIRE SPECIES, NOT WITHOUT MORE BURRITOS! WE'RE USELESS TO YOU WITHOUT THEM!

Doctor Thorn leaned toward him, visibly intrigued. Darren's nose plugs failed to filter out the sheer intensity of the Weed's curiosity.

"Tell us more about these . . . burritos."

CHAPTER FIVE

"Doctor Thorn!" a Stink Weed scented loudly. He was planted in front of a control panel that looked like an air conditioner. "The mother ship is demanding a report on our status."

An irritated aroma escaped the alien commander. "Tell them that we've experienced minor technical difficulties. But be careful how you smell. Don't let them get a whiff of what we've become—or they'll try to Decontaminate us and turn us back into weak, insipid Flowers!"

Doctor Thorn reeked of disgust at the very idea of becoming a Star Flower again.

"Now then, where were we?" the Weed said. "Ah, yes, you said something about burritos. Speak quickly, mammal!"

Darren swallowed hard.

WELL, he farted, IT ALL BEGAN IN THE SCHOOL CAFETERIA, SEVERAL WEEKS AGO. . . .

He quickly explained how the radioactive burritos had transformed four ordinary kids into the Fart Squad. I MEAN, EVERYBODY ON EARTH FARTS NOW AND THEN, BUT OURS ARE REALLY SOMETHING.

MINE ESPECIALLY, Tina farted with pride.

AND WE CAN'T FART WITHOUT THE BURRITOS, Darren stressed.

"Fascinating!" Doctor Thorn rubbed his vines together. "Tell us where we can find these miraculous burritos—and the rest of your so-called Fart Squad!"

FORGET IT! Darren said. He just wanted to keep the Stink Weeds from carrying him and Tina off into space. I'M NOT TALKING UNTIL WE'RE BACK ON SOLID GROUND!

"And then what?" Tina whispered, using her actual voice.

"No clue," Darren admitted. "I'm making this up as I go along."

Tina sighed. "I was afraid of that."

"Do not test my patience, meat-creature," Doctor Thorn reeked. He wrapped a spiky vine around Darren's neck. Thorns jabbed Darren's skin. "You are in no position to bargain with us. Tell us where to find what we want or you and your stunted companion will suffer!"

DON'T KNOCK IT, Tina farted indignantly. MY HEIGHT IS KEY TO THE WHOLE SILENT MYSTIQUE I'VE GOT GOING.

Darren's upset stomach roiled furiously.

A monster fart demanded to be let free. He couldn't hold it in anymore—and wasn't sure he wanted to. He tugged down the translator shorts to let it rip.

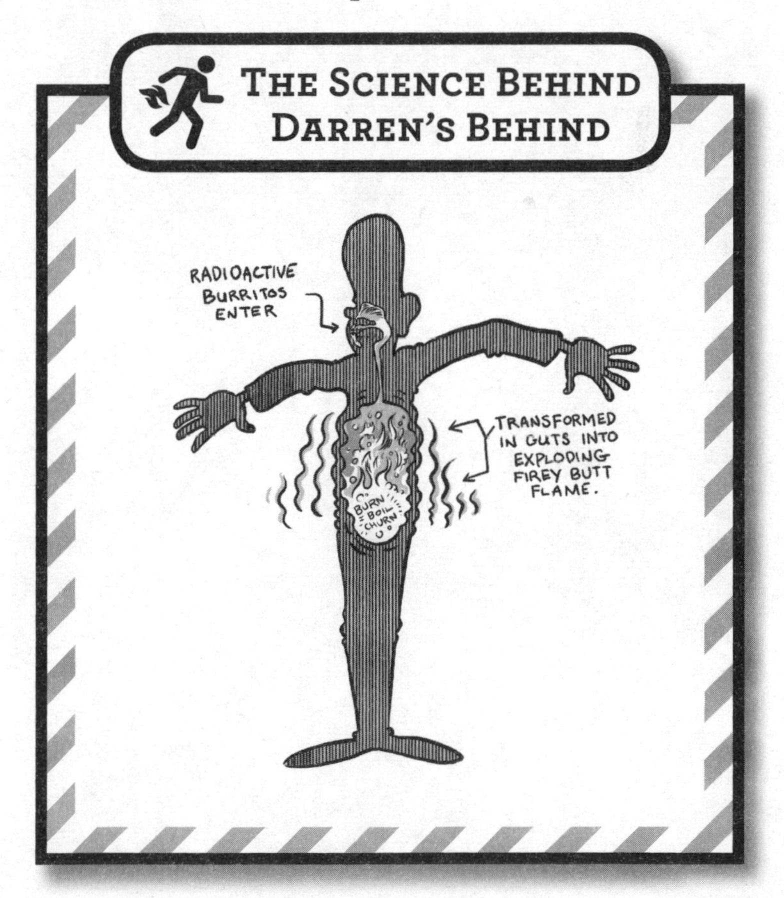

"Fire in the hole!"

A volcanic *blaaat* erupted from his butt, singeing the seat of his pants. A deafening boom shattered the glass walls of F.A.R.T.S., causing the UFO's pressurized atmosphere to whoosh out through the broken windows. Loose pieces of equipment were sucked out into the open air. Darren and Tina had to grab on to a steel examination table to keep from getting sucked out of the ship. The Stink Weeds rooted themselves to the dirt floor, even as the gas from Darren's fart caused them to mutate even more. Oozing sap dripped from fresh vines and thorns sprouting all over their bodies. The Weeds twitched and shook.

"Miserable human!" Doctor Thorn stank angrily. "What have you done to my ship?"

Sparks exploded from the control panels. The UFO began spinning out of control and diving toward Earth.

"We're losing altitude!" a Stink Weed reported frantically. "We're going to crash!"

Tina looked at Darren. She shouted over the roaring winds from outside. "No offense, but I'm not sure you really thought this through!"

"Tell me about it!" he said.

CHAPTER SIX

"Hold on!" Darren shouted as the UFO plummeted toward the ground below. Clinging to the examination table for dear life, he saw through the shattered windows that the ship was heading straight for the farmlands outside Buttzville. Open fields seemed to rush up at him with frightening speed.

"Brace for crash landing!" Doctor Thorn ordered his crew. "Deploy emergency brakes!"

Jets of smelly exhaust blasted from the

bottom of the ship to cushion its landing . . . sort of. The UFO skidded across a leafy cornfield, sending everything and everybody in the lab flying. Stink Weeds crashed together, getting tangled in one another's vines, which were still growing feverishly, thanks to Darren's high-volume fart. The sunlamps on the ceiling exploded. Darren flinched and ducked his head to avoid the shower of sparks.

"Oomph!" he grunted.

The impact knocked the wind out of him. It took him a moment to realize that the UFO had come to a stop and he was still alive. He looked around anxiously.

"Tina?"

"Over here." She climbed to her feet nearby. Her hair was a mess and her clothes dirtier and more wrinkled than they had ever been before, but she was still in one piece, more or less. "Next time you blow up a spaceship, a little more warning would be appreciated!"

"Sorry," he said. "That one kinda got away from me!" He picked his sore body off the ground as fast as he could and tugged the translator shorts back up, just in case.

"Quick! Let's make a break for it while we still can!" he called out to Tina.

"Right behind you," she said. "I never want to look at a weed again!" Darren checked to make sure the Stink Weeds were still tangled, then helped Tina out a broken window before hopping down to the ground below. The UFO had crashed into a cornfield on the outskirts of town, digging a deep trench in the dirt. Darren spied a farmhouse, barn, and silo ahead. A motorized hay baler was parked in front of the barn.

"Run for it!"

But Doctor Thorn and the other Stink Weeds were right behind them, pouring out of the crashed spacecraft. "After them!" the Botanican scientist scented loudly. "Don't let them get away!"

The Weeds chased Darren and Tina through the rows of corn, the aliens' spiky vines growing faster than ever. Looking back over his shoulder, Darren saw the weeds gaining on them. Tina took out her phone as they ran.

"What are you doing?" he asked.

"Texting an SOS to the Squad!" she said. "What else?"

The vines nipping at their heels, they raced out of the cornfield toward the farmhouse. Then a harsh voice shouted at them.

"Hey there! What's all this racket?"

A scowling farmer emerged from the barn, holding two snarling hound dogs on leashes. The dogs strained to break free, snapping and barking. Foam sprayed from their jaws.

"You kids don't belong here!" the farmer said, glaring at the intruders. "No trespassing!"

"Help!" Darren shouted. "We're being invaded by Stink Weeds from outer space!"

Oddly, the old farmer did not immediately believe Darren. He didn't budge from where he stood, blocking the kids' escape. The dogs snarled and drooled.

"Don't be smart with me, boy! Crazy kids and their pranks!"

"But you have to believe me!" Darren said. "They're right behind us!"

"I'm not falling for your tricks . . . !"

"Oh, for goodness' sake," Tina said. "We don't have time for this."

A stealth fart rustled her uniform. The farmer's eyes rolled backward and he keeled over into a pile of hay. The dogs whimpered briefly and passed out a moment later.

"Pleasant dreams," Tina said sweetly.

But before they could start running, the Stink Weeds came slithering out of the cornrows. Stinging vines grabbed Darren and Tina. Thorns snagged their clothes and skin.

"Hold on to them at all costs!" Doctor Thorn ordered the other Weeds. "We still need them—and their precious burritos!"

So much for our great escape, Darren thought. *The Weeds have got us again!*

CHAPTER SEVEN

"Take them back to the ship," Doctor Thorn ordered. "The mammals failed to permanently disable our engines. Prepare to activate the backup fertilizers!"

Caught by the vines, Darren squirmed uncomfortably. Was it just his imagination or were the thorns even sharper than before?

"It's not fair," Tina complained. "We almost got away."

"At least they haven't gotten the burritos yet," Darren said. "That's something, I guess."

The Stink Weeds began to drag the kids back toward the cornfield. Darren was trying to figure out what to do next when a familiar voice shouted from above.

"Chill out, everyone!" Juan-Carlos yelled. "Here we come!"

Darren looked up in surprise. The rest of the Fart Squad was flying to the rescue, propelled by Walter's fart-powered jets. Juan-Carlos perched on his flying friend's shoulders, while Walter seemed to be using the GPS on his phone to track down the location of Tina's phone.

"Watch out!" Darren shouted at his friends. "They're after you and Walter . . . and the burritos!"

"Silence!" Doctor Thorn reeked. "Order your friends to surrender at once!"

NO WAY, Darren tooted. MY SQUAD NEVER GIVES UP. JUST LIKE FARTS, YOU CAN'T KEEP US BOTTLED UP FOREVER!

He just hoped his friends knew what they were doing.

Walter dropped Juan-Carlos off in front of the barn, just out of reach of the aliens' vines. Juan-Carlos looked a bit spooked, but tried to talk tough.

"Listen up. Let go of our friends and this doesn't have to get, well, uglier than you are." He gave Darren and Tina a puzzled look. "Hey, why are you wearing aluminum underwear?"

"Never mind that!" Darren shouted.

"These Weeds are trouble. They want to kidnap us all and take us back to their home planet!"

"Seize the foolish human!" Doctor Thorn said, although Darren realized that only he and Tina could understand the Weeds.

Jaws snapping, a couple of Stink Weeds charged at Juan-Carlos. Darren fought to free himself, but could only watch helplessly as the mutated aliens went after his friend. If only he could use his fart abilities without making the Weeds even stronger . . . !

"Uh-uh," Juan-Carlos said, scrambling backward. "We're ready for you this time!" He hollered up at Walter. "Whack those weeds!"

"Acknowledged," Walter said. "Providing air support now!"

Tooting through the sky, he performed a loop-the-loop high above the farm. Darren noticed for the first time that Walter had a pair of Super Soaker squirt guns strapped to his back. Walter reached around and took hold of the squirters.

"What the heck?" Darren wondered aloud.

He watched hopefully as Walter swooped down over the charging Stink Weeds like a very pudgy crop duster, squirting them with something that made them wilt and turn brown around the edges. The startled Weeds shrank back in fear, losing their grip on Darren and Tina, who broke away from the twitching vines and ran to join Juan-Carlos. Frantic smells sounded like shrieks in Darren's nose, overpowering the peculiar smell of the spray, which he couldn't quite place.

"Way to go!" Juan-Carlos said, cheering Walter on. "Keep it coming!"

Darren's hopes began to rise. "What's he spraying them with?"

"Weed killer, of course," Juan-Carlos replied. "My dad's secret recipe. One half vinegar, one half dish soap. Works every time."

Of course, Darren thought. *What else would you use against weeds?*

Pollen sprayed from the Weeds as they tried to bring Walter down, but he was too high up. Darren worried briefly about the unconscious farmer and his dogs, but figured they were safe enough where they were. The Weeds were after the Fart Squad right now, not some random farmer.

Lucky us, he thought.

Darren grabbed a pitchfork from a nearby haystack. The Weeds were obviously not giving up. Although slightly wilted, they sank their roots into the rich soil of Earth, refusing to retreat.

"Don't surrender!" Doctor Thorn ordered his crew. The weed killer was holding them back for the moment, keeping them confined to the cornfield, but it was only slowing them down. "We're Weeds. Nothing can stop us from spreading!"

And then Walter's squirt guns ran dry. . . .

The twin sprays dwindled to trickles. One last squirt emptied Walter's supply. He was all out of weed killer—and the Stink Weeds were still standing.

Juan-Carlos gulped. "Er, does anybody have a Plan B?"

"I wish!" Darren said.

CHAPTER EIGHT

"We will have our revenge," Doctor Thorn vowed, uprooting himself from the ground. A furious stench radiated from his wilted brown petals. Walter's amateur crop-dusting had not improved the Weeds' mood any. They lurched after the kids, chasing them across the farm. "You will all pay for your paltry attempts to poison us!"

"Now what?" Juan-Carlos asked, running beside Darren and Tina.

"I don't know!" Darren turned to fend off grasping vines with his borrowed pitchfork. These alien Weeds were even more stubborn than the ones in his mom's garden. "But running away isn't enough. If we can't stop them here, they'll infest the whole planet!"

An idea hit him.

He recalled how the Star Flowers had detected the Fart Squad from all the way out in space, as well as how Doctor Thorn had tried to hide his crew's transformation from his fellow aliens. Maybe he could use his translator shorts to send an urgent warning to the Botanican mother ship, alerting them to Doctor Thorn's nefarious plan to turn their entire species into Stink Weeds.

"Juan-Carlos!" Darren asked. "Do you have any burritos on you?"

"You bet!" Juan-Carlos lobbed a squashed foil package to Darren, who caught it one-handed. "Figured you guys might need to refuel."

Darren quickly unwrapped the burrito. It was cold and greasy and unappetizing, but now was no time to be picky. He needed to stuff his stomach with gas if he was going to pull off what he had planned. This couldn't be just any fart. It had to be a fart that could be smelled from space!

"Seize the specimens!" Doctor Thorn smelled loudly. "And do not be gentle about it!"

The Stink Weeds were getting faster and stronger as the effect of the weed killer wore off. Tina scrambled behind the parked hay baler to get away from an angry Weed, while Juan-Carlos knocked over a large, cylindrical bale of hay to buy Darren some time. Walter hurled his empty water guns at the Weeds from above.

"If you're going to do something, Darren," Juan-Carlos said, "you'd better do it quick!"

Darren had to agree. He crammed the revolting burrito into his mouth and practically swallowed it whole. Gooshy beans and spicy sauce hit his stomach like gasoline on a fire. His gut churned volcanically, the pressure instantly building up inside him, demanding release. He struggled to hold it in while dialing the volume on his translator shorts as high as it would go. His lips quietly mouthed a warning as he farted urgently:

A fart to end all farts went off in his shorts, testing the limits of the alien underwear. His butt burning, Darren could only hope that, somewhere out in space, his message would be received.

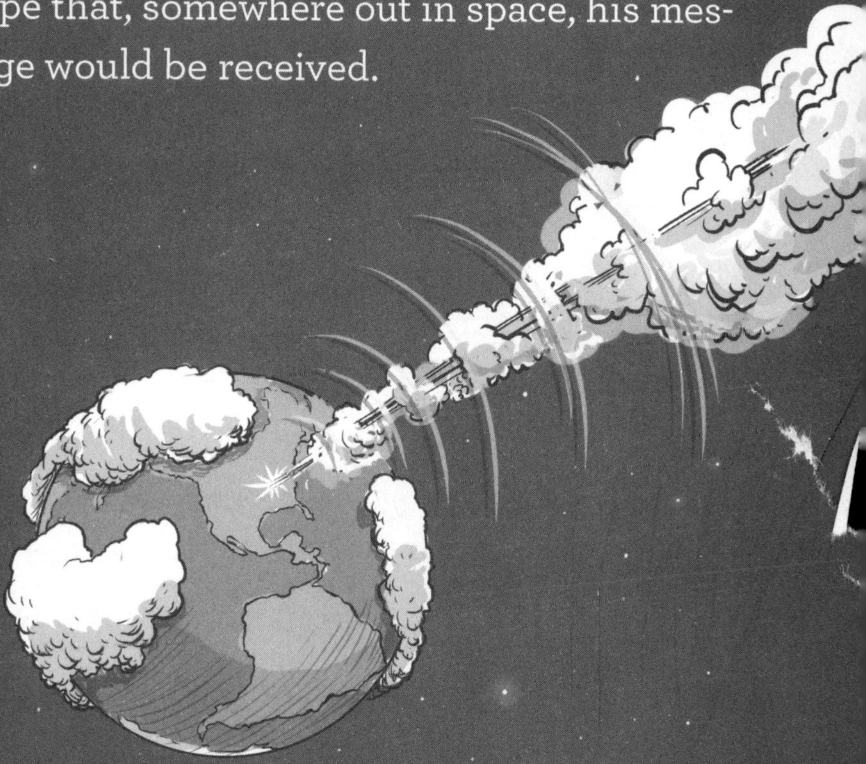

If not, Earth's future would be full of weeds!

CHAPTER NINE

Darren's emergency fart did not go unnoticed by the Stink Weeds.

"No!" Doctor Thorn smelled in dismay. "If those Goody Two-shoes Flowers find out about us before we're ready—"

A sonic boom shook the sky, followed by the overpowering smell of fertilizer. A bright white glare lit up the isolated farm—as a humongous UFO arrived at the speed of smell.

The gigantic F.A.R.T.S. was at least ten times bigger than the Stink Weeds' crashed scout ship. It hovered hundreds of feet above the cornfields. An intensely floral perfume gushed from the UFO's loudsmellers.

"Attention: Mutant Plants! Prepare for General Decontamination Wash."

"Never!" Doctor Thorn stank defiantly! He shook his thorny vines at the ship. "We're Weeds now. We don't want to be cured!"

"Your thought processes have clearly been impaired," the mother ship responded. "Remain still and allow yourself to be scanned so that we can isolate the cause of your mutation."

But the Stink Weeds refused to cooperate. "Retreat!" Doctor Thorn ordered. "Back to the ship! We can still escape from those irksome Flowers—and stay Weeds forever!"

The Weeds slithered frantically back toward their own UFO, seeking refuge from the Star Flowers and a means of escape. Darren realized that he couldn't let them get away. He knew from his mom's garden just how hard it was to get rid of weeds for good.

The other Star Flowers can't do this alone, he thought. *It's up to me to deal with these weeds, once and for all!*

He hopped into the seat of the mechanized hay baler and fired up its engines. "Out of the way!" he shouted at his friends as he hit the gas and chased after the fleeing Weeds. As he suspected, the Weeds were weakened by the weed killer and could not outrun the speeding piece of farm equipment. "Time to wrap this up, in more ways than one!"

"No!" Doctor Thorn smelled in alarm. "Halt your infernal contraption! We must get away from those Flowers—before they turn us back into what we were!"

"Sounds like a pretty good idea to me," Darren said.

He bounced atop the baler as it ran over the Weeds, scooping them up into the baling mechanism, which rolled them into tight, leafy tubes wrapped in twine. One by one, the baled Weeds were pooped out the

back of the baler, landing with a thud on the ground.

"Wretched meat-monsters!" Doctor Thorn rolled across the farm, his bound vines packed into the shape of the bale. "Release us!"

NOT A CHANCE, Darren tooted. WE'VE FINALLY GOT YOU WEEDS UNDER CONTROL.

He called to the rest of the Squad, who helped him roll the captured Weeds back under the hovering mother ship.

OVER TO YOU, he farted.

"Thank you, mammals," the Star Flowers responded. "Decontamination procedures can now commence."

"Stop!" Doctor Thorn protested. "Don't do this to us!"

The Weeds twisted and strained, but, bound in bales, their vines were tied. A bright golden beam from the UFO scanned them for a minute or two, while Darren and

his Squad crossed their fingers that the other aliens would be able to fix the Weeds. Sprinklers protruded from the bottom of the ship.

"Commencing Decontamination."

The sprinklers activated. A sudsy wash, which smelled like lemons, drenched the Weeds, who began to *change* once more. The spray washed away the jagged petals and thorns and turned the plants' stems supple and green again. The snapping jaws closed, while fresh yellow petals bloomed in the glow of the hovering mother ship. Doctor Thorn threw up his shrinking vines to protect himself, but it was no use. The Decontamination spray seemed to reverse the mutation caused by the original farts. Within minutes, the Stink Weeds were gone, replaced by a half dozen beautiful Star Flowers.

"Much better!" Tina nodded in approval. "I was really getting tired of those hideous weeds."

"You and me both," Darren said, but he wished for another burrito as the tallest of the Star Flowers glided toward him. After that big, long-distance fart, he wasn't sure he had another one in him. "Doctor Thorn?"

"Call me Professor Blossom," the transformed alien scented. He smelled like perfume now instead of stinking like a weed.

"Doctor Thorn seems a bad dream now."

"You can understand me? I don't have to fart-speak anymore."

"Now that I'm no longer a weed, there's no need. Let me offer my most sincere apologies for our terrible behavior before."

"No harm done," Darren said, choosing to overlook an abduction and attempted invasion. He held out his hand again. "Perhaps we can start over?"

As far as he knew, there weren't any more stink bombs waiting to go off.

"I'm afraid not," Professor Blossom said, dipping his petals sadly. "Your planet is obviously too hazardous to our kind. From now on, we will keep our distance from Earth, so that the Stink Weeds will never return."

Juan-Carlos shrugged. "I can live with that. Considering."

"I concur," Walter said. "Better safe than sorry."

The Fart Squad watched as the restored Star Flowers boarded the mother ship, which hooked a tow chain to the crashed UFO before taking off back into the sky. Darren craned his neck, following the rising ship

until it vanished into the clouds. All that was left behind was scattering of loose petals and thorns.

"Good-bye and good riddance," Walter said. "That's one way to dispose of unsightly and invasive flora."

Juan-Carlos sighed in relief. “I’m just glad they’re leaving without us.”

“But I was right all along,” Darren couldn’t resist pointing out. “There really was an Unidentified Farting Object.” He smirked at Tina. “I think somebody owes me an—”

He toppled over in midsentence, landing flat on his back.

“I’m sorry,” Tina said. “Were you saying something?”

⁂ ⁂ ⁂ ⁂ ⁂

The sun was already setting by the time Darren made it back home. He was going to be late for dinner, but not as late as he would have been if the Stink Weeds had gotten their way.

Good thing I'm not halfway across the galaxy by now!

At the last minute, he remembered to peel off the translator shorts and chuck them in the recycling bin before heading inside. Even still, his mom took one look at his scratched face and dirty clothes and gasped out loud.

"Darren! What on earth have you been up to now?"

"Nothing much," he answered. "Just a little weeding."

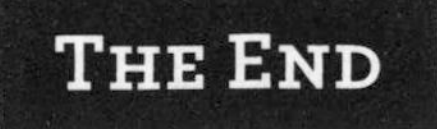

Read a Sneak Peek of Book Four, *Fart Squad: The Toilet Vortex*

CHAPTER ONE

"I think I'm going to be sick," Darren Stonkadopolis groaned as he backed away from the toilet.

Janitor Stan leaned over his shoulder to get a better look at the offending specimen. "Oh, you're fine," he said. "Happens all the time." And with the push of one finger, Stan flushed that toilet good.

Stan was the only human being whom Darren and his friends trusted to keep their identity as the elusive superhero team, the Fart Squad, a secret. He also doubled as their coach, or scent-sei. Cleaning up toilets after school wasn't exactly how Darren would have chosen to demonstrate his gratitude. But when Stan asked Darren for help with a running toilet, Darren just couldn't say no.

"Okay," Stan declared to the otherwise empty bathroom, "which one of you won't shut up?" He eyed the row of toilets before pointing to the far end. "Aha, gotcha!" he announced.

Darren followed the janitor to the last stall. "No water on the floor," Stan said as they stopped in front of it. "That's good." He pushed the stall door open, and Darren shivered. Suddenly it was really, really cold.

Stan grabbed the toilet handle and tried jiggling it. The water kept running, forming a swirling vortex in the center of the bowl. He lifted the lid off the toilet's tank and peered inside. "Everything looks okay," he told Darren, "but sometimes something gets knocked loose." The janitor reached inside the toilet's tank and fiddled with a valve, but the water kept on running.

"Nothing there," Stan said, pulling his arm from the tank and drying it on a rag from his back pocket. "Could be something clogging the actual toilet pipe, I guess. What's weird is the toilets up here have been doing this all week—every time I get one to stop, another starts acting up." He studied the toilet bowl and the water swirling down into it before finally sticking his hand in there.

"There's definitely suction," he reported. "A whole lot of it, actually. In fact"—his shoulder twitched and wrenched, but his hand was still in the toilet—"I think I'm stuck!"

"What?" Darren grabbed the janitor's free hand and tried to pull him loose. It didn't help. Then the rushing-water noise got louder, and suddenly Stan jerked forward, his arm in as far down as his shoulder.

"There's definitely something wrong with this toilet!" Stan said, bracing both feet against the toilet base and pulling with all his might. But he couldn't get his hand back out. And now more of his arm was being pulled down into the toilet! It was like the toilet was a monstrous mouth swallowing up the janitor!

"It's no use. I'm going down!" Stan shouted, struggling against the pull. Darren tried tugging him free again. Still no success.

There was a scuffling noise as Stan's feet left the ground, his shoulder and part of his chest in the toilet bowl now. Then, with a loud slurp, his head and upper body disappeared down the pipe, as well.

"No!" Darren cried, tugging on Stan's leg. A second later Darren lost his grip as Stan's legs went, and the toilet swallowed the janitor completely. His wrench made a loud clang as it fell to the floor by the toilet, after which the bathroom was quiet except for the rush of water running. "Stan!" Darren shouted into the toilet.

"Help!" Stan shouted, sounding very far away.

"Stan!" Darren called again. But this time he got no answer—

"STAAAAAAAAAAAAAAN!"

BLAST OFF WITH . . .
FART SQUAD
FART SQUAD
SEAMUS PILGER
STEPHEN GILPIN
FART SQUAD
FARTASAURUS REX
SEAMUS PILGER
STEPHEN GILPIN
FART SQUAD
UNIDENTIFIED FARTING OBJECTS
SEAMUS PILGER
STEPHEN GILPIN
HARPER
An Imprint of HarperCollinsPublishers
www.harpercollinschildrens.com